This edition published by Parragon in 2009
Parragon
Queen Street House
4 Queen Street
Bath BA1 1HE, UK

ISBN 978-1-4075-8184-2

Printed in China

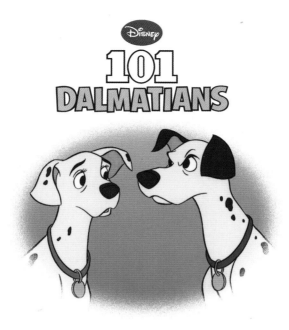

101 DALMATIANS

Adapted by Mary J. Fulton • Illustrated by Don Williams

Bath · New York · Singapore · Hong Kong · Cologne · Delhi · Melbourne

In a small house in London, there lived two happy couples: Pongo and Perdita and their humans, Roger and Anita.

Pongo and Perdita were the proud parents of fifteen Dalmatian puppies.

And Nanny, the housekeeper, was there to look after all of them.

One day, the nasty Cruella De Vil came to buy the puppies
and wouldn't take no for an answer.

"Perdita would be heartbroken," said Anita.

"Nonsense!" snapped Cruella. "I want those puppies."

"We're not selling the puppies," said Roger. "And that's final."

"You'll be sorry!" shouted Cruella.

It was getting late, so Pongo and Perdita tucked the puppies into bed. Nanny agreed to puppy-sit while the older dogs went out for their usual evening walk with Roger and Anita.

Cruella De Vil had hired two crooks, Jasper and Horace, to steal the puppies. "We're here to inspect the wiring and the switches," Jasper told Nanny.

"We didn't call for any inspection. You're not comin' in here," said Nanny.

But Jasper and Horace pushed past her. They quickly put the puppies in a carpetbag, ran out the door and escaped.

When they got home, Pongo, Perdita, Roger and Anita were heartbroken. They called the police and the newspapers. But the next day, the puppies were still missing.

"Perdita, I'm afraid it's up to us," said Pongo. "We'll try the Twilight Bark. It's our only chance."

The Twilight Bark was the way dogs spread news. Later, when Pongo and Perdita went for their walk with Roger and Anita, the dogs barked a desperate message into the air. "Fifteen spotted puppies stolen. Have you seen them anywhere?"

Pongo's message was barked from dog to dog. It travelled through London, where it was picked up by the Great Dane at Hampstead. Finally, it reached the countryside and the ears of the Colonel, a sheepdog who lived in a barn. His friend, a cat called Sergeant Tibs, was with him.

"Hmmm," muttered the Colonel, perking up his ear.
"Fifteen spotted puddles – stolen!"

"It sounds like puppies, Colonel, sir," said Sergeant Tibs.
"Two nights ago, I heard barking over at the De Vil mansion."

"No one's lived there for years," replied the Colonel.
"We'd better investigate."

The Colonel and Tibs arrived at the De Vil mansion and sneaked in through an open window. Once inside, Tibs squeezed through a hole in the wall.

"Why, there's a whole roomful of stolen puppies here!" Tibs exclaimed. There were ninety-nine pups all together.

"We must contact the parents," said the Colonel to Sergeant Tibs as they hurried back to the barn.

As soon as the news got back to Pongo and Perdita through the Twilight Bark, they set out for Hampstead.

There the Great Dane gave the Dalmatians directions to the Colonel's barn. "The Colonel will show you how to get to the old De Vil place," he said.

"De Vil!" said Perdita with a gasp. "I hope we're not too late!"

Meanwhile, at the barn, Sergeant Tibs and the Colonel spotted a
car speeding toward the De Vil mansion. "We'd better see what's
up," said the Colonel.

Once inside the mansion, Tibs couldn't believe what he heard.
Cruella De Vil planned to make fur coats out of the puppies!

"The police are everywhere," snapped Cruella. "I want
this job done tonight – or else!"

Luckily, the crooks wanted to finish watching their television show first. Sergeant Tibs rounded up the puppies quickly and quietly. The show ended just as the last puppy disappeared through the hole, followed by Tibs.

"The pups flew the coop!" shouted Jasper.

Tibs and the puppies scrambled all around the mansion. But wherever they went, the two crooks were right behind.

Finally, Tibs and the puppies were cornered. "We've got 'em now!" Jasper said, gloating.

Then, in the nick of time, Pongo and Perdita came crashing through the window and attacked the crooks.

"Quick, kids!" shouted Tibs. Out through another hole in the wall they went, running for the barn just as fast as their puppy legs could carry them.

Struggling to get free, Jasper and Horace stumbled into a wall. Down came the ceiling plaster, right on their heads. And out the window went Pongo and Perdita.

When all the Dalmatians were safely in the Colonel's barn,
fifteen happy puppies jumped all over Pongo and Perdita, while
the rest shyly watched.

"Why did Cruella want so many puppies?"
wondered Perdita.

Then Tibs told them about Cruella's wicked plan.

"Fur coats!" cried Perdita. "What'll we do?"

Just then the crooks' truck pulled up outside. "We'll take *all*
the puppies back to London with us," said Pongo. "And we'd
better get going right now!"

It was a long, hard trek. Finally, the Dalmatians came to a village, where they hid in a blacksmith's shop. A friendly Labrador arranged a ride to London for them in a van.

But Cruella and the crooks had followed the dogs' tracks to the village. Cruella parked her car right beside the van.

"Oh, no!" cried Perdita, looking out the shop window. "How will we get to the van?"

The answer to Perdita's question came from two puppies wrestling in the fireplace. Covered with soot, they looked like two little Labradors. "That's it!" shouted Pongo. "We'll roll in the soot. We'll all look like Labradors!"

A parade of black "Labradors" marched to the van, right under the nose of Cruella De Vil. Their plan might have worked, too – if a blob of snow hadn't fallen off the roof onto the last puppy, washing away the soot.

"After them!" Cruella shouted to Jasper and Horace as Pongo leaped aboard the van with the last puppy clenched in his teeth. The van roared down the road toward London.

Cruella in her car and the crooks in their truck went in hot pursuit of the van.

But the van sped away and – *CRASH!* Jasper smashed into Cruella's car.

"You idiot!" Cruella shouted at Jasper as she jumped out of her car. She stood in the wreckage and watched helplessly as the van continued on its way to London.

In the small London house, Roger and Anita and Nanny were sadly sharing some tea. Suddenly the door burst open and a pack of excited black dogs tumbled into the room.

"Where did all these Labradors come from?" asked Anita in amazement.

"They're not Labradors at all!" said Nanny, dusting the soot from one of the puppies. "Look!"

"The puppies!" cried Roger. "And Pongo!"

"And Perdita!" said Anita as the room filled up with puppies. "Oh, Roger, whatever will we do with them all? If I counted right, we have one hundred and one Dalmatians!"

"We'll keep them," said Roger. "We'll buy a home in the country. We'll have a plantation."

"Yes," Anita said with a laugh. "A Dalmatian plantation!"

"It'll be a sensation," Nanny said.

And as Roger began to sing about it, all one hundred and one Dalmatians barked in happy agreement.